The Sankofans

The Sankofans

Rom Wills
Wills Publishing

The Sankofans

Copyright 2006, 2014
By
Romuald P. Wills

Romuald P. Wills
romwills@aol.com

ISBN-13: 978-0615977447
ISBN 10: 0615977448

To my sons.

ONE

"There was another food riot in Maryland," Shelly said as she walked to the couch and sat down with Thomas.

Thomas Hunter was half engrossed in the sex scene of the primetime reality show, *One Night Stand*, where a camera crew filmed people meeting at bars and going home to have sex. "Another one?"

Shelly sucked her teeth. "Why must they fight over food? They could just buy it like we do."

"Maybe they can't afford it. So many people are out of work and the subsidies only take people so far."

"Well they need to get jobs."

"Jobs where? Everybody isn't like us."

"I know. They're lazy bums. Those Black people are an embarrassment."

Thomas glanced at Shelly's chocolate skin, straight hair by way of a relaxer and green contact lens. "They're not like us huh?"

"There are haves and have-nots. We're haves. You know that," Shelly said. She looked at Thomas's copper skin, and rugged face. She had chosen wisely especially with his financial portfolio. "Why are you so concerned about them? It's not like you came from them. Your parents had money before they passed away. You didn't come from those people."

"Perhaps. Still, I have distant relatives who are among those people. I just feel that in different circumstances that could have been me."

"It isn't you. You're not lazy. You have an education and a career."

"Maybe some of 'those people' as you call them would have did the same thing if they had the same circumstances. I mean really. Can it all be put on their shoulders? Black people lost everything during the depression of 2012. The world itself still hasn't recovered."

"That's no excuse. People like us have careers. We have everything we want. They're just using their circumstances as an excuse to be lazy."

Thomas looked at Shelly intently. On paper and on the surface they were compatible. They both came from upper middle class families. They both had postgraduate degrees. They were able to make it in corporate America despite the repeal of Affirmative Action programs in 2017. Most importantly their financial portfolios matched, particularly the all important credit scores. Despite the similarities Thomas felt something was missing.

He took Shelly by the hand and stood up. "You're right. There is no excuse for laziness. Forget about that. This show got me hot."

"I know that look in your eyes mister," Shelly teased. "Sex wasn't on the schedule for tonight."

Thomas winced. Something about how Shelly spoke. "Let's be spontaneous for once."

Shelly thought for a second. "Sure, why not?"

TWO

Thomas sat in his office staring out the window. He had come far in corporate America as a financial officer with MagnaCorp, one of largest corporations in the world. He looked at his office, his awards, and tailored suits as badges of his talent and ambition. He was a Black man who wasn't stopped by what his father called a "glass ceiling." Things like that didn't exist in 2032. Anybody with the talent could make it to the top. He didn't, however, see many faces like his unless they had a Spanish accent.

It was in stark contrast to what he saw every day on his drive to work from his gated community. Every day he drove past homeless people and dilapidated buildings. The faces of the people he saw had lost hope. Most of them had their belongings in shopping carts. "Those people" as Shelly had called them were part of the sprawling Black underclass. There had once been a more stable Black middle class but that was decimated by the depression and the rollback of Affirmative Action.

Everybody wasn't homeless. There were still Blacks working in jobs in megastores like Wal-Target or even in corporate America as support staff.

Of course there were people like him and Shelly who were growing scarce.

"You all right, Thomas?"

Thomas turned around to see Malik come into the office. Malik delivered mail throughout the building. "I'm okay. How's it going for you?"

"Can't complain. Every day I open my eyes it's a good day."

Thomas looked at the locs that framed Malik's face. He always wished he could get away with growing locs. "You're always in a good mood."

"I strive to maintain my peace."

"Hmmmm." Thomas had a faraway look in his eyes. "I wish I had that sometimes."

A slight smile crept on Malik's face. "You ever been to a poetry reading?"

"No."

"There's a reading at Afrikan Renaissance this Friday."

"Afrikan Renaissance?"

"It's a bookstore in Northeast." Malik reached in a bag in his mail cart and took out a flier. "Here ya go."

Thomas took the flier and examined it. "I haven't heard of this place."

"Many people haven't. Those who know…know. Check it out this Friday. You'll enjoy yourself."

"I think I will."

THREE

Thomas couldn't help feeling something was out of place as he drove to the poetry reading at Afrikan Renaissance. At first he was reluctant because of the neighborhood. People said that it was a poor area, which meant it was mostly Black. It wasn't what he expected. Growing up as he did in a gated suburban community he wasn't exposed to the inner city nor was he exposed to people from those areas. His only impression came from news reports and his parents who were relieved to be away from that environment.

Of course, he would have to drive past poor neighborhoods to get to work but they were the ones visible from the main roads and highways.

What he was seeing was different. For one thing the neighborhood was clean. There wasn't even an odd candy wrapper on the streets. The row houses were in good, even great condition. What really opened his eyes were the people. They were Black people but there was something different about them. They walked prouder and with purpose. It was similar to how Malik at the office walked. There were many people with locs. Their clothing was even different. The clothing had Afrikan designs. The people didn't look like they were from Afrika. They appeared to be Black Americans just like him.

He noticed how the people behaved around each other. This was something he hadn't seen before. It wasn't the guarded behavior of the underclass nor was it the stiff behavior of the Black Bourgeoisie. There was an openness in how they interacted with each other.

Thomas made it to Afrikan Renaissance. Thomas thought it was interesting that the sign for the store spelled Afrikan with a "K". He would ask about it later. It was a good size building with a small parking lot. Thomas pulled into one of the last spaces and parked his car. Even though his late model Jaguar was the most expensive in the lot he felt it would be safe. He was strangely at peace as he got out of the car.

He walked into the store where he saw an array of books, incense, and clothes. A clerk greeted him as he walked past the sales counter.

"Peace brother."

Thomas was caught by surprise. "P-peace...um...hi."

"This is your first time here?"

"Yeah. What gave me away?"

"Our regulars walk through like they own the place. My name's Lamar." He extended his hand.

"Thomas Hunter." Thomas shook Lamar's hand.

Lamar regarded Thomas' fish out of water demeanor. "So what brings you to our fine establishment?"

"A guy on my job gave me a flyer. His name is Malik."

"Ah yes. Brother Malik. You work for MagnaCorp?"

"Yes I'm a Financial Officer."

"Good work for you bruh?"

"It's a very good career. I couldn't imagine doing anything else," Thomas said unconvincingly.

"Well brother, go through the door to your right." Lamar indicted the door. "Welcome home."

Thomas looked at Lamar briefly. "Thank you."

Thomas walked through the door and was hit with the smell of incense. He looked around at the several people sitting at tables. The people looked regal in their colorful Afrikan garments. As Thomas found the only empty table he admired the different natural hairstyles worn by the women in the café. There was something different about the women on another level. At the moment Thomas couldn't quite put his finger on it.

Thomas looked around the room a bit before focusing on stage and that's when he felt a twinge in his stomach.

She was beautiful. She had a slim face with full lips and a button nose. Her locs were long and full, reaching down to the small of her back. The green and white dress she wore complimented her smooth chocolate skin. She was quite shapely. She had just finished a poem judging from the response of the audience.

"Asante Sana," the woman said to the audience. "Y'all want one more piece?"

The audience clapped its approval.

"I'm feeling the luv. This last piece is personal. It's about duality in ourselves and in the people we choose to love."

She drew a deep breath and then began speaking.

Who are you?

Who are you?
When I met you,
I saw light
Now I know you,
I see darkness
Who are you?

Who are you?
I see light
I see darkness
I see both
Co-existing in your soul
Who are you?

Who are you?
The light is bright
It shines for all
Darkness is there

It engulfs all
Who are you?

Who are you?
You have the power of creation
To bring peace
You have the power of destruction
To bring strife
Who are you?

Who are you?
You are good
You are evil
You project peace, comfort
You project fear, destruction
Who are you?

Who are you?
Harbinger of Hope
Angel of the Abyss
Who are you?

Who are you?

Who are you?

The audience clapped in appreciation. An MC appeared on stage.

"Thank you, Sister Ayanna. We'll be taking a break for a bit. Stretch your legs and get something from the juice bar and we'll be back in twenty."

Thomas watched Ayanna as she walked to his table and took a seat.

"Greetings brotha. Are you enjoying yourself so far?"

"I am. I enjoyed your poem."

"Thanks. Thank you for keeping my bag company."

Thomas saw the bag on the floor under table. No wonder she sat down next to him he thought.

"I would have sat down next to you anyway," Ayanna said, as if she read Thomas's mind. "I like meeting new people."

"What do you do besides read poetry?" Thomas asked.

"This is it for me. I have a few spoken word vids out."

"I wasn't aware people did poetry vids."

"It's not like they are in the rotation on MVHBET-ONE. Most spoken word vids are about positive growth. The mass media seems to promote trash like that *Hump The Booty* mess."

"I've seen that one." Thomas didn't want to say he loved that particular vid.

"The elders say that vids like that would not have been shown before the Patterson, Dickerson et al vs. the FCC case back in 2021 which allowed for pornography to be shown on any channel. Now you can't find anything positive on television. It's a good thing I don't watch."

"How do you make money if you're not on the vid channels?"

"Fortunately I have other avenues to promote myself."

"How? I thought the corporations controlled everything."

Ayanna smiled. "Not everything. At least not what really counts."

Thomas was about to ask what she meant when a voice called out to him.

"Thomas you made it out!"

"Malik." Thomas stood up to shake Malik's hand.

"Baba Malik!" Ayanna stood up to give Malik a warm hug. "Please have a seat."

Malik sat down. "Thanks for coming out Thomas. Are you enjoying yourself?"

"Have to say that I am."

"Well you're not the only one." Malik winked at Ayanna.

Ayanna nudged Malik's shoulder playfully. "Stop playing Baba."

"Stop blushing sis," Malik laughed.

There was something in the exchange that Thomas picked up on. He just wasn't sure what it was.

Ayanna looked up at the stage. "They're about to get started."

Thomas spent the rest of the evening enjoying the company of Ayanna and Malik and thought provoking poetry.

FOUR

"Peace Brother Thomas. Thanks again for coming out," Malik said as he dropped off mail at Thomas's office.

"Peace...Brother Malik." Thomas responded hesitantly at first. It was the first time he referred to someone as *brother*. "I enjoyed myself."

"That's good to hear. You have to come out again. Ayanna would really love to see you."

Thomas was confused. "I thought you two were together."

"Naw bruh. We're just close like that."

"Really." An image flashed in Thomas's mind of him and Ayanna relaxing on a grassy hill.

Malik recognized the look on Thomas's face. "Sister Ayanna is at the Renaissance every Friday. You should come check her out."

"I think I will."

"Well bruh, they don't pay me to sit around on the plantation. I'll see you tomorrow. Peace."

As Malik walked out, one of Thomas' coworkers, Ward McWhorter, walked in. Ward was an inch taller and shade darker than Thomas.

"Were you actually having a conversation with the mail carrier?"

Thomas noted the disgust in Ward's voice. "Malik? We were talking about this place I visited last week, Afrikan Renaissance."

Ward looked surprised. "You fraternize with the help?"

"Is there a problem with that?"

"No, if you like talking with low IQ people."

"How do you know Malik has a low IQ?"

Ward looked surprised. "He wouldn't be a mail carrier otherwise. If you want to fraternize with him that's on your shoulders. Who knows? He might be motivated to better himself." Ward paused for a second. "What's this I heard you mention about Afrikan Renaissance?"

"It's a spot over in Northeast."

"I actually know a lot about that store," Ward said arrogantly. "Afrikan Renaissance is a chain of stores throughout the country."

"I had never heard of them. How do you know about them?"

"The owners and the clientele follow so-called Afrocentric beliefs."

"I read about Afrocentrism in school. There was a big debate about that philosophy in the early part of the century."

"A debate the Afrocentrics lost. They were thoroughly discredited. Their only lasting legacy is Kwanzaa, which only a few people celebrate anyway."

"So how do you explain Afrikan Renaissance? I went there last Friday and there were plenty of people there."

"Apparently, the Afrocentrics went underground. They certainly weren't in the news. Whatever the case, pockets of them are still around. I had a friend named Scott who worked in the government. He had it all: job security, a home, and a wonderful girlfriend with the most beautiful blond hair and blue eyes. Then for whatever reason he started going to Afrikan Renaissance to buy books.

"I started to notice a change in his behavior. He began criticizing society and questioning everything. He broke up from his girlfriend. We were out one time and we saw this Black woman with dreadlocks and no makeup. She was dark and ugly…she repulsed me and I told him. He almost hit me for calling her ugly. Our friendship became strained.

"One day he stopped by and told me that he resigned from his government position and had sold all of his belongings. I thought he was crazy. I told him few Black men had the type of life he had. He just looked at me and smiled. He left my condo. I thought for a second and then ran out after him. I saw him get into a car. Fortunately I was parked on the street, so I got in my car and followed him to Afrikan Renaissance. I watched him go into the building with a couple of men. I got out and went inside. I pretended like I was looking around but I couldn't find him anywhere. After that I hired a private detective to look into that business. He told me what could before he disappeared. I decided to leave the place alone."

"They seemed cool with me."

"That's how cults get people."

"I thought they were just a business? When did they become a cult?"

"They have to be something. Both Scott and that detective became more militant before they disappeared. Stay away from those people. They're dangerous."

Thomas thought about how Ward sounded like Shelly when he said, *those people*. "I'll be the judge of how dangerous they are." Thomas had an image of holding Ayanna's hand.

"It's your life!" Ward said.

"Yes it is," Thomas responded.

FIVE

"You've been quiet tonight. Is anything wrong?"

Shelly looked intently at Thomas as they were finishing their dinner at *Marco's*, one of the best restaurants in the DC area for upscale Blacks. Thomas looked up from his half-eaten food to answer Shelly.

"Everything is okay. Just some work-related stuff." Thomas thought about his conversation with Ward McWhorter earlier.

"Well you need to relax," Shelly put her hand on Thomas's hand. "We have a big night ahead."

Thomas thought ahead to their scheduled night of sex. The thought of Shelly looking at him with her green contacts didn't appeal to him at that moment. The waitress interrupted his thoughts.

"Would you like to see a dessert menu?"

Thomas looked up at the waitress who was wearing locs and had a smooth mocha brown complexion. She reminded him of the women at Afrikan Renaissance. "Nothing for me, thank you. How about you Shelly?"

"Not tonight," Shelly said with a slight sneer.

"Would you like your check then?" the waitress asked.

"Give us a few minutes," Thomas said.

Shelly sucked her teeth when the waitress walked away.

Thomas wondered why all of a sudden Shelly had an attitude. "What's wrong with you?"

"Why would they hire somebody like her?"

Thomas was perplexed. "What's wrong with her? She's been providing top-notch service all evening."

"Oh her service has been great but look at her."

Thomas shrugged.

Shelly sighed. "She has an…Earth mama, crunchy granola bar look. I mean, wearing dreadlocks in a place like this and wearing those weird earrings. I'm surprised she has hasn't been fired."

"For having locs?"

"Yes. I mean, look around the room."

Thomas scanned the room. He saw Black men and women looking beautiful, wearing expensive clothes and looking like the most important people in the world. Then all of sudden an insight struck him. These people were putting on facades. Sure they looked good but their behavior was that of people hiding behind masks.

He looked at the men with their fancy suits and cell phones in hand. They were conspicuous in their arrogant banter.

He looked at the women with their pressed hair and color contacts projecting an air of manufactured sensuality.

Why hadn't he noticed before?

Then an image popped in his head of the men and women at Afrikan Renaissance. They wore their hair natural and proudly. They wore their Afrikan garments without a hint of pretense.

The men stood tall and proud, projecting true strength and power.

The women were naturally sensual and feminine. The source coming not from a pre-packaged item on a mega-supermarket shelf but from the very essence of their being.

Then at that moment Ayanna popped into his mind. Her beautiful chocolate skin glowed like a miniature sun.

He looked at Shelly who had the same exact complexion but whose light seemed dim by comparison.

He knew instantly that something was wrong with the reality he lived in.

"Are you okay Thomas?" Shelly was genuinely concerned. "You look like you drifted off there for a second.

"I'm fine," Thomas lied. "Let's get the check. I'm ready to go."

SIX

"Greetings Brotha Thomas." Ayanna embraced Thomas warmly as he entered the café section of Afrikan Renaissance. "How has your week been?"

"It's been interesting. Sis – Sister Ayanna. My eyes have been opened to many things."

"Things such as what?" Ayanna sat down at an open table and watched as Thomas joined her.

"Just looking at the façade this world presents. I was at a restaurant last night with my…um… girlfriend." Thomas expected a visible reaction from Ayanna. When her facial expression didn't change Thomas continued. "The…sister waiting on us had locs and though she provided exemplary service, my…girlfriend had problems with her because of how she looked."

Ayanna raised her left eyebrow. "How did she look?"

"Well…" Thomas thought for a second. "She looked like she would fit in better here than at *Marco's.*"

"*Marco's*!?! Did the sista have on 'Gye Nyame' earrings?"

It was Thomas's turn to raise his left eyebrow. "Gye Nyame?"

"It's an Adinkra symbol from Ghana." Ayanna pointed to the symbol on the far wall of the café.

"Yes she had earrings like those."

Ayanna laughed. "I know her, Imani. Your girlfriend wouldn't want to mess with her. Imani was a gang member before she came to us."

Thomas mentally took note of the statement, 'before she came to us.' He decided to take the conversation in another direction. "You know, one of my co-workers warned me to stay away from this place. In so many words he called it a cult."

Ayanna's demeanor became serious. "A cult? Where would your friend get an idea like that?"

"He said he knew someone who became more militant after buying books here. The person eventually disappeared."

"Tell me more about your friend."

"Ward? He's just an average brother. Well…I don't know about the "brother" part. Even other brothers on the job call him an Uncle Tom. He probably wouldn't feel comfortable here. He didn't have a favorable view of Afrocentrics."

Ayanna looked puzzled. "Afrocentrics? Oh, that's the term used years ago. We for the most part call ourselves Afrikans."

"Africans, but you are all Americans aren't you?

"We're citizens of a political entity called the United States of America but by our DNA and ancestry we're Afrikans."

"That's in line with what I read about Afrocentricism. I thought the movement had died out. Apparently it went underground."

Ayanna chuckled. "Many people thought we went underground. We never went anywhere. If anything we got stronger."

"Really. My co-worker, Ward, said that Afrocentricism was discredited."

"You can't discredit the truth. The mainstream media suppressed information about us, especially around the depression. While many people in the middle class were losing everything, Afrikans were creating businesses and other institutions and thriving. We had our own economy. Corporate layoffs weren't an issue with us. This wasn't something that other races or even the Black middle class wanted to hear.   So we were largely ignored. Your co-worker is conservative right?"

"Yes."

"Black conservatives never know what was going on in the Afrikan community anyway. Nothing's changed in that regard."

Thomas nodded. "That's something. You'll have to excuse me. I need to use the restroom."

"Hurry up. The set is about to start."

Thomas went to the restroom in the basement going over in his mind everything Ayanna had said. There were Afrocentrics, no, Afrikans who were building institutions and thriving. A smile crept on his face as he relieved himself, washed his hands and walked out, almost running into a group of people in the hallway.

"Excuse me," Thomas said as he surveyed the group.   A brother with short locs and Afrikan clothing led them. Thomas had seen him in the poetry café. The three women with him looked different. They didn't have locs or Afrikan clothing. The women had permed hair and though they had on casual clothing, they looked to be members of the Black Bourgeoisie. He also noticed that the three women had small backpacks with them.

"Excuse us brotha," the man leading the group said. They continued walking to a door at the end of the hallway. The man produced a key and opened the door, allowing the women to walk through, and walked in himself after giving Thomas a brief look.

Thomas stood there with the feeling that something significant had just happened.   He wondered about the significance as he returned to the café.

Thomas sat down at the table with Ayanna. "Are you familiar with everything at Afrikan Renaissance?"

Ayanna smiled. "This is like a second home for me."

"Really? There's a door downstairs past the restrooms. A brother and three sisters went through the door which locked behind them."

"They were probably having some type of meeting."

"I don't know. I didn't get the feeling they were going to a meeting. The three sisters had backpacks and they didn't look particularly Afro…Afrikan to me."

"What do you think they were doing?"

"I don't know. I was hoping you could tell me. One thing I found interesting is the bird symbol on the door. The bird was picking something off of its back. Something about the bird touched me."

"You saw a Sankofa bird."

"Sankofa?"

"It's one of our most precious symbols. The word 'Sankofa' is from a proverb from the motherland, Ghana to be precise. Sankofa means that it is not taboo to go back to the past in order to move forward. Many of us have retrieved our Afrikan heritage in order that we may move forward as a people."

"Like a journey?"

"Exactly."

"Those sisters looked like they were going on a journey. Where do you think they were headed?"

"They were going someplace," Ayanna said knowingly. "The set is about to start, we can talk later."

Thomas only half paid attention to the poetry as he thought about the door with the Sankofa bird.

SEVEN

"Brother Thomas, how ya feeling today?" Malik asked as he walked into Thomas's office.

"I'm feeling fine.   I was at Afrikan Renaissance this past weekend."

"Starting to feel at home huh?"

"I do feel comfortable there. By the way, where's your cart?"

"I'm on a break right now."

"Have a seat." Thomas indicted the leather couch.

"I have a few minutes." Malik sat down. "So you really like the Renaissance?"

"I'm really impressed brother. Very professional operation. I was reading some information about Afrikan Renaissance on the WorldNet. I didn't know it was such a large chain. There are well over one hundred stores ranging from tiny stores in malls to a couple of superstores. I didn't know that many people supported Black bookstores especially those with Afrikan themes. I read an article in *Black Life* magazine that such bookstores were extinct."

"*Black Life* caters to what's left of the, no offense, Black Bourgeoisie. Yeah *Black Life* is really out of touch with Black life. It should be called *Colored White Life*."

Rom Wills

"Now Malik, I don't know if that's fair. *Black Life* has many great articles. One example is a recent article about the state of the economy and the lack of opportunities for the Black poor and working class. That's something that affects all of us."

"The economy affects all of us but in different ways." Malik leaned forward. "You know, you have two groups of Blacks in this country. You have one group, who cling to Eurocentric culture. They are the corporate Blacks making six figures, living in gated communities, and driving the latest Korean car.

"There are also the Blacks who live on some type government assistance or live as wage slaves.

"And of course you have the homeless living in cardboard boxes under the freeways or squatting in abandoned buildings.

"That's one group. The other group is the Afrikans who live a different type of life."

Thomas interjected. "You seem to suggest a difference between Blacks and Afrikans."

"Hundreds of years ago there wasn't a difference," Malik said. "Anybody can be born Black. That Black person at some point must make a conscious decision to become Afrikan."

Thomas raised his eyebrows.

Malik continued, "For Afrikans or as we also call ourselves, Sankofans…"

"I was just introduced to the concept at the store. Oh sorry for interrupting."

"No problem. For Sankofans the economy is irrelevant because we support ourselves. We need very little from the greater community. Take the Afrikan Renaissance store chain. There are over a hundred stores providing jobs for a couple of thousand Sankofans. The mere presence of the chain creates other jobs as well. The stores provide an outlet for book and magazine publishers, vid companies, disc companies, and even clothing companies. Sankofan companies. These publishers, vid producers, and clothing companies use Sankofan printers and manufacturers who in turn get raw materials from Sankofan companies in the States or in Afrika. That's just one area.

We have our hands in everything that's important to not only sustain ourselves but also to thrive."

"You know," Thomas said. "Ayanna said something similar. She also said that most people don't want to see those types of accomplishments by Afrikans."

"Unfortunately even other Blacks don't want to see Afrikan accomplishments. There are those who have more faith in others than in themselves."

"Who has more faith in others?" Ward McWhorter walked in as if on cue.

"Hi Ward," Thomas said.

"Thomas." Ward looked at Malik. "Shouldn't you be working? You don't want to lose this job. You probably couldn't get a job like this anywhere else." Ward chuckled to himself.

Malik stood up slowly and looked Ward dead in the eye. "Brother. Don't ever speak to me like that again."

Ward blinked a few times and stepped back. "I-I-I'm not your brother."

Malik stared at Ward for a tense filled moment. "You're right. You're not my brother, Ward. Every brother ain't a brotha."

"What makes you think you can call me by my first name? That's Mr. McWhorter to you. How do you know my name anyway?"

"You told me to call you Ward when we met years ago."

"We met? I don't hang out with…people who look like you."

Malik laughed. "We met at a Young Conservatives Conference at Hopkins in the spring of '22."

"Were you serving food?" Ward asked in all seriousness.

"Actually, I was giving the keynote address."

Ward thought for a second, "I remember a speech by a Black Conservative named James Mason. You're not…" Ward looked at Malik more closely. "How?"

"You know him?" Thomas asked Ward.

Ward looked at Malik. "Are you James Mason?"

Malik smiled. "I used to be."

Ward looked at Malik intensely. "How did you get into this Afrocentric mess? You had been working with a major conservative think tank. How did you end up here?"

"I wouldn't call the "Afrocentric" thing a mess. Let's just say I was offered a better deal."

"But to end up pushing a mail cart? Even if you became Afrocentric you can do better than this. You were very smart."

"There is purpose in everything. I have my reasons."

"Why then?"

"I could tell you but I only share my reasons with my brothers."

Ward glared at Malik and walked out.

Thomas looked at Malik. "You used to be conservative?"

"Yeah, we all stumble on the path."

"Why are you here? Ward seemed to suggest that you could be doing other things besides pushing a mail cart."

"I could be. Who's to say that I don't? Why am I here at this time? At this moment? Perhaps to help others find the path. I have to go back to work. We'll talk again."

Thomas closed his door behind Malik and sat down. More questions. Ayanna. Malik. Afrikan Renaissance. Sankofa.

EIGHT

"You have a faraway look Thomas." Shelly was concerned as she and Thomas walked to the theater to see the latest stage play, *Mother Dear Gets a Life*.

"Just thinking about some things," Thomas said as his mind drifted to the events of the past few weeks. He felt like his eyes were being opened to a new aspect of life.

"You've been distant lately mister. You need to relax."

"Yes, you're right."

"I know I'm right. I...tch." Shelly looked disgusted by something she saw.

"What's wrong now?" Shelly's moods were beginning to irritate Thomas.

"Over there." Shelly pointed to a group of homeless people in the direction they were walking. They were standing by a truck where some men and women were handing out food. "Why don't they get jobs?"

"Shelly you know why they don't get jobs. They can't get what's not there." Thomas immediately thought about what Malik said about the Sankofans.

"There are jobs out there. They are just too lazy to get them."

"Shelly I don't feel like going down this road with you."

As they got closer Thomas saw that the people handing out food had locs and one of the men had a Sankofa bird tattooed on his neck. As they walked past the group Thomas felt compelled to speak to the man.

"Peace brother," Thomas said to the man with the Sankofa tattoo. "Are you with Afrikan Renaissance?"

The man regarded Thomas coolly. "Naw brotha I don't work there. What do you know about the Renaissance?"

"I've been there a few times to..." Thomas caught himself. He remembered that Shelly was with him. "To check out the books. The place was recommended by someone on my job named Malik."

"You work for MagnaCorp?"

"Yes."

"Oh okay." The man relaxed a bit. "My name is Kofi." Kofi extended his hand to shake Thomas's hand. "Like I said we don't work for the Renaissance. We're the Afrikan Homeless Advocacy Organization. We work with the homeless as far as getting them food, clothing, and shelter. We do a few other things as well."

"That's great. It's good to see someone doing something."

"Thomas," Shelly interrupted. "We have to get ready to go. The play is going to be starting soon."

Thomas was a little irritated by Shelly's behavior. "In a minute." Thomas turned to Kofi. "I see what you're doing out here and it makes me realize I need to be doing more."

"If you're going to Renaissance you'll probably find some way to help. Have you been through the door yet?"

"No."

"Do you know what door I'm talking about?"

"The door with the Sankofa bird on it?"

"Yes. One day you'll walk through it. Until then stay on the path. Peace Afrikan."

"Peace," Thomas said as he turned to continue to walk towards the theater.

After a block of silence Shelly turned to Thomas. "Why did he call you an African? You're an American. Why didn't you say something?"

"Don't worry about it Shelly."

"That was a funny play," Shelly said as she and Thomas walked through the door of her Arlington, Virginia townhouse.

"It was okay," Thomas said distantly as he sat down.

Shelly sighed as she sat down next to Thomas. "You've been behaving differently lately. I'm not sure I like the change."

"What don't you like?"

"You seem to be showing a lot of interest in this African stuff. It's crazy. All that stuff belongs back in the 1960's. Black men and women were wearing their hair without relaxers. I saw the pictures."

Thomas looked at Shelly with her green contacts and freshly permed hair. "I've seen the pictures as well. I see people with natural hair and think it's beautiful. The natural beauty of Afrikans is awesome." Thomas surprised himself with how comfortable he was with his statements.

"We're not Africans!!! Don't say that!!!"

"You're right. Someone has to make a choice to be Afrikan."

"Oh you're claiming to be African?"

"Maybe." Thomas stood up. "Have you ever wondered if there was more to our lives? We've been reduced to numbers in a system. A man and woman will meet and instead of just enjoying each other's company they will discuss their resumes and credit scores. Character means nothing. Purpose means nothing."

"What's wrong with credit scores? How can anyone make it without good credit? You can't get a job, a house, or a car. You can't even get food in most stores without good credit unless you're one of those poor people who still use cash. This system requires credit. If you want to live in this system, there is no alternative."

Thomas thought about Afrikan Renaissance. "Maybe…maybe we don't know all the options."

Shelly was livid. "There are no options! Are you crazy!" Shelly composed herself. "Thomas I don't know if this is going to work out. It seems like we are going in different directions. I'm not getting younger. My schedule was to get married in another year. My goal is to marry an educated Black American with a great career and great credit. Not someone who thinks nappy hair is beautiful and being African is something in which to be proud. I need to find that man."

Thomas looked at Shelly and felt sorry for her. "It was good knowing you." He began walking towards the door.

Shelly was surprised. "Just like that? You're not going to try to work it out?"

"We want different things. You want a Black American man. In a moment of clarity I realize that I want to be an Afrikan. Peace."

Thomas let himself out of Shelly's townhouse into the night air without looking back.

NINE

Thomas took his time as he walked around the neighborhood surrounding Afrikan Renaissance. He got off work early just so he could really explore the community. It was a warm spring day; so many people were out laughing, going about their business, talking about politics. It struck him that most of the people seemed to have at least one book in their hands. In fact, one small park in the neighborhood had several people of different ages ranging from the late teens to elders sitting either alone or in groups, reading and discussing books.

Thomas chuckled to himself as he recalled several articles in the media claiming that Blacks didn't read. Maybe Blacks didn't read but Afrikans sure did.

Thomas walked back towards Afrikan Renaissance. For the first time he paid attention to the stores that surrounded the bookstore.

There was a raw food café, a gourmet Vegan restaurant, a juice bar, a grocery store, two clothing stores, and even a theater. Every single store was crowded and the theater had a long line to see a movie called, *The Conscious Ones.* He didn't recall that movie being mentioned on the Previews Channel. He definitely planned to check it out when he got a chance.

He had begun to walk back towards Afrikan Renaissance when he realized that something was missing from the picture he had been viewing: children! Where were the children? The youngest Afrikans he had seen were in their late teens. Even their manner and demeanor was older than their years. Yet another mystery from people that seemed to be full of them.

Thomas walked into the bookstore and greeted a few people he recognized by face until he ran into Ayanna. After they embraced Ayanna suggested they have a seat in the outdoor section of the store.

Thomas didn't waste any time with his questions.

"Ayanna what's the real significance of the door with the Sankofa bird. I have a feeling you haven't told me everything."

"Hmmmm," Ayanna smiled. "I see your third eye is opening."

"Third eye?"

"I'll explain later. The door is called the *Door of the Return*."

"Door of the Return?"

"In Senegal, there is a door called the *Door of No Return*. Afrikans were herded through this door before being put on the slave ships. It was their last time in Afrika."

"Does the *Door of the Return* represent the journey back to Afrika?"

"Not a physical journey, though many of us have returned to the motherland. It represents a return to who we really are. In many ways our Sankofa. We are…Sankofans."

"Malik mentioned that term. I…I think I want to become a Sankofan. I want to walk through the door." Thomas surprised himself with his boldness.

Ayanna looked at Thomas intently. "Do you know what you're getting into? Once you go through that door there's no turning back. You're not even going to want to come back. Do you know what's on the other side?"

Thomas chuckled. "You know, I really don't know. I just feel with every fiber of my being that's it's home."

"Very well then." Ayanna stood up. "I'll be back."

Ayanna returned with the brother who took the three sisters through the Door.

"Thomas. This is Eshu. He'll discuss what you need to do to go through the Door. If you'll excuse me." Ayanna walked away.

"So Thomas, you want to join our family?"

"Yes."

"Even though you know very little about us?"

"I've been to the store several times and like what I've seen."

"You want to change your life because you like a little bookstore?" Eshu asked in a harsh tone.

"It's more than that," Thomas sighed. "I just don't like where I'm at now."

"You think this is a career change? You're talking about changing your life. Once you go through that door do you think you're going to go back to your gated community? Do you think you you're going to still be driving that nice Jag? Or chilling in your plush office? Or boning that self-hating girlfriend of yours? Oh wait…y'all broke up."

Thomas was surprised. "How…"

"Brotha, an ant can't pass through our community without us knowing everything about it. Nothing or no one escapes our notice. We've survived for so long for a reason."

"I'm serious, I want to do this."

"You are willing to sacrifice everything?"

"Everything?"

"Maybe even your name."

"My name?"

"Yes your name." Eshu decided to ease up on Thomas. "Look brotha, I see in your eyes that you're sincere but sincerity is not enough. You have to be committed mind, body, and soul. This is what I need you to do and once you have done this I will take you through the Door."

"What do you need me to do?"

"You need to quit your job and sell all of your possessions

37

including your home and car. Sell all of your stock and liquidate your investment portfolio."

"I guess I give you that money?" Thomas was beginning to think that this might indeed be a cult.

"Good question. We encourage critical thinking. You will put that money into a savings account, preferably in a bank that's Black owned, either one of them." Eshu allowed himself a rare chuckle. "It's still your money. We don't need it but you will want another house and car and investments…in different areas. When you are ready, call this number." Eshu took a card out of his wallet and handed it to Thomas. "You will hear a beep. When you hear the beep, say clearly, "open the door." The next day at exactly 9:00 pm you need to be sitting in the lecture room in the store. All you need is the clothes on your back and maybe a backpack with some personal items special to you such as family pictures. Then and only then will I take you through the door. Do you have any questions?"

"No."

"Okay." Eshu stood up. "Oh, one more thing. Until you make the call, do not visit Renaissance or any other business you think is Afrikan–controlled."

"Why?"

"I don't want you in our world until you are ready to break with your own world. You can't have a foot in both while you're making your decision."

"I understand."

"Good." Eshu turned and walked away.

Ayanna appeared as if out of nowhere. "Thomas, I hope to see you on the other side."

Thomas looked at Ayanna thinking about how beautiful she was. "I hope to see you there."

TEN

Thomas stared into space as light jazz played in the background. It was his favorite disc by *The Hanson Group*. Thomas looked at the blue eyed, blond hair band. He recalled overhearing someone at Afrikan Renaissance talk about how jazz was started by Blacks. It was hard for Thomas to believe. He loved Jazz but he didn't recall seeing a Black jazz musician.

Thomas missed going to the bookstore. It had been a week since he had been there. He had many things to think about.

Thomas looked around his townhouse. Not many people could afford to sit where he did in a multi-million dollar home. He had beautiful furniture and all the latest electronics including the new 3D holographic video system.

In his garage he had a '31 Jaguar, which he bought to replace his '30 Mercedes. He thought about getting a Korean car, which seemed to be the rage lately. Maybe he wouldn't be getting a new car after all.

His credit score was in the highest percentile and his salary was in the mid six figures. He was a financial executive with a Fortune 5 company with a multimillion-dollar stock portfolio.

After his breakup with Shelly his profile automatically listed his relationship status as single on the WorldNet dating services. Women from all over the world were sending their pictures and credit scores.

Rom Wills

Thomas Hunter had everything.

He really had nothing.

Thomas felt a hole in his spirit. No, not a hole, a hunger for something more out of life, out of society. What did a poet at the store call it? The Machine Culture.

Indeed it was a Machine Culture. Everything was about numbers and profits fitting into a mathematical pattern. A zero and a one.

How did it get this way?

Thomas thought back to early childhood in an upper middle class gated community outside of DC. As a time when the economy was failing and jobs were being shipped overseas, his parents were living very well. Thomas's father worked as a contractor with the military, which stayed busy with wars in the Middle East, Africa, and South America.

His mother worked as an administrator with the county school system.

His life was in direct contrast to the homeless population or the working poor. Even the middle class was suffering. Then the Great Depression of 2012 hit and everything got infinitely worse.

Thomas and his family didn't suffer. Nor did their social network. While people were having trouble making ends meet, Thomas and his friends were riding in private boats in the Bay. While people were having trouble keeping cars running his family was buying a new car every year. While people were barely having full meals, Thomas was gorging himself at the functions of his social set. Then tragedy struck.

First his mother died of breast cancer while he in high school and then a few years later his father was killed while doing contract work in the Middle East during the Iranian Conflict. Despite this Thomas was able to live his life as he always had.

He graduated with other like-minded Blacks from Howard University, which in the early twenties was one of the few Historically Black Colleges that actually had a Black majority. Then he got an

MBA from Georgetown. He got a job immediately with MagnaCorp and began moving up in the ranks to his current position.

He had everything that a Black man, indeed any man could want. So what was missing? Immediately Ayanna popped into his mind. He smiled thinking about her natural radiant beauty. He felt good just being in her presence. Her smile, her personality, her beauty, her...life.

Her life.

Malik's life.

Eshu's life.

The life of everyone at Afrikan Renaissance.

The life of the Afrikans around Afrikan Renaissance.

Life!!!

That's what's missing from his life.

It was sterile.

It was mechanical.

He felt alive with the Sankofans.

He had not felt like this before.

Not growing up in a household where his parents showed little affection towards him or each other.

Not growing up where his so-called friends seemed to spend more time comparing the accomplishments of their parents than actually enjoying their own lives.

Not working in a corporate environment where making profit caused people to lose their very humanity.

He had lived his life in a machine culture. Now he was ready to leave.

To really live.

Thomas picked up his cellphone and dialed the number of his real estate agent. When her freckled face appeared on the tiny screen, Thomas didn't waste any time.

"Diana, I want to sell my house."

ELEVEN

"You must be crazy! Why would you leave this job!?! Ward was livid as he watched Thomas delete his private files off of his MagnaCorp computer. Thomas's once plush office only had a desk and a chair as Thomas had already sold or given away everything in the office that belonged to him. "You must be crazy!"

"You said that already." Thomas had on a lightweight sweatshirt, jeans, and athletic shoes. He had a small backpack by the door.

Ward couldn't believe what was happening. "Why? Why? Don't tell me those Afrocentrics got to you? You would throw all of this away to hang out with people trying to be something they are not. Something you are not. Y'all not Africans!!!"

Thomas finished deleting files and stood up. "It's getting late, Ward. I have to go."

"Are you going to Afrikan Renaissance? Are you joining that cult?"

Thomas smiled. "It's an Afrikan thing. You wouldn't understand."

"What..." Ward didn't know what to say as he watched Thomas walk out. Ward already watched the Renaissance trap two people. He wasn't going to fail another one.

Ward was ready this time. He parked on the street where he could see Thomas come out of the building. He knew Thomas would have to turn his badges in at MagnaCorp Security. Ward waited maybe ten minutes before Thomas tried to hail a cab that passed him by. Two more cabs passed Thomas before one stopped for him.

"It figures," Ward said when he saw that the driver had locs. Ward pulled his car into traffic to follow the cab.

TWELVE

Thomas saw three other people in the lecture room when he walked in, two sisters and a brother. One sister reminded him of Shelly. She had on light brown contacts and pressed hair. She looked like she was one of Shelly's sorority sisters.

The other sister had a different look. Her hair was braided with what looked to be extensions. She had a hard demeanor with several tattoos on her arms.

The brother was something else. His clothes were dirty and disheveled. Amazingly he didn't have an odor like many homeless people he came across. Despite his appearance, Thomas saw a light, even a wisdom in his eyes. Thomas thought he probably had an interesting story.

The four sat in silence until the door to the lecture room opened at exactly 9:00 pm. Eshu walked in and surveyed the room. In a stern voice, Eshu said, "Follow me."

The four people followed in silence as they walked through the bookstore seemingly oblivious to the many people in there.

Ayanna watched as Thomas followed Eshu. A tear of happiness came to her face, as she knew what awaited Thomas. She remembered when she walked through the door in what seemed like a lifetime ago.

Many thoughts went through Thomas's mind as they walked through the store and began walking down the steps to the door. He thought about everything that happened to bring him to this point. Every step he took he thought about everything he gave up to have life.

As they walked to the door Thomas felt engulfed by a warmth around his body. He felt sense of peace.

Eshu reached the door and without fanfare took out his key and unlocked the door as casually as someone unlocking the door to his house. Eshu opened the door wide and motioned everyone to walk through. Thomas was the first to enter. He was surprised that the hallway was empty, except for lights. There was another door at the end of the hallway. This door had the *Gye Nyame* symbol on it. Thomas opened the door into the back yard, which had what looked to be a small moving van. Thomas and the others looked back at Eshu who motioned them to get into the van.

The four got in and Eshu closed the door behind them and hit the back of the van three times. The van driver started the engine and pulled out of the back yard.

Ward watched from a vantage point where he could see the van. Those Afrocentrics aren't so smart Ward thought. After Scott disappeared Ward figured the Afrocentrics must take people out a back door. It was easy to find, Ward thought as he got to his car. The van wouldn't be able to get too far. Ward pulled out his parking spot and saw the van pull out of the alley.

Ward smirked. He would follow them to their compound, report them to the authorities, save Thomas and Scott, and be a national hero. Ward had a vision of doing press conferences, talk shows, and national magazines. He could have his choice of beautiful blondes from the reality TV show, *Bang That Slut*.

Ward's thoughts were interrupted when he was rear ended by an old model car from depression years. Furious, Ward watched as the van pulled away. He got out of his car and saw who rear-ended him. A younger Black man with loose clothing and braided hair. First the

Afrocentrics and now one of those Hip Hop guys. Hadn't Hip Hop died during the depression? "You ran into my car!"

The young man got out of his car. "Hey man, I'm sorry. Oh dag man. I messed your ride up. I must not have been paying attention." The young man used his hands as he talked. "Yo, you know I was talking to my girl on my cell, you know. She got a little phat booty. She got that thing going. You know what I'm saying?"

Ward noticed the young man put his fist out for a pound. Ward left him hanging. He was disappointed that the van had disappeared. Fortunately he had a friend at Homeland Security. Ward turn to the young man. "Do you even have insurance?"

The young man smiled showing gold teeth. "Yeah, yeah, yeah man, you know I got insurance. You know I'm a law-abiding citizen. But yo…" The young man started to sound philosophical. "The booty on my girl is phatter than a government subsidy. I think the subliminal thought of my girl put me into a … a…a trancelike state which took my mind out of the present thus not alerting me that I was about to run into your ride. All I can say is…my bad."

Ward sighed. He really thought those Hip Hop types were extinct. "Let me get your insurance information. This is an unfortunate accident."

The young man pulled out an envelope with some papers in it. "I don't know man. It's all a matter of perspective. Unfortunate for one man is fortunate for another one."

Ward stopped and looked at the young man's face intently as he wrote down his insurance information. So intently that Ward didn't notice that the young man's shirtsleeve rolled up a bit revealing a Sankofa tattoo.

THIRTEEN

"Hey brotha, we're here."

Thomas had drifted off to sleep. He opened his eyes to see the homeless brother gathering his plastic bag of belongings and following the two sisters out of the van.

Thomas got to his feet and followed the others out of the van. Thomas surveyed the surrounding area. It was still night. His watch read 4:17 in the morning. They were parked in front of a big house sitting on at least an acre of land. He could make out a few more houses. There weren't any streetlights so it was hard to make out anything else. A voice caught his attention.

"Brothers and sisters. Welcome to Garvey."

The voice belonged to a tall sister who looked regal in her Afrikan clothing and gray locs that reached down past her shoulders. She spoke with a motherly authority.

"My name is Auset. My assistants and I will ease your transformations. You will be guided to your rooms in what will be your home for the next month. Your sisters will guide you. Welcome home."

The women behind Auset stepped forward and embraced each of the newcomers. The sista who embraced Thomas had a healthy but curvy body with a round pleasant face that radiated compassion.

"Greetings brotha Thomas. My name is Akua. I will be assisting you the next twenty-four hours."

"How do you know my name?"

"The same way we know everything. Let's go to your room."

Thomas followed Akua into the house and upstairs to one of the bedrooms. Akua opened the door and turned on the light, allowing Thomas to walk in. The room had a painting entitled *Triple M Brilliance*. The painting was of Marcus Garvey, Malcolm X, and Martin Luther King. The only other things in the room were a desk, a chair, a night table and a bed. There was also a plastic bag by the desk. There was also a pair of clippers on the desk as well as a towel.

"What are the clippers for?" Thomas asked, already suspecting the answer.

Akua smiled mischievously. "I know you worked long and hard to get those waves just right." Akua sighed dramatically. "But they gotta go. Snip, snip, my brotha."

Thomas couldn't help but laugh. "I knew my life was going to change but not the waves. What will the ladies think?"

Akua plugged in the clippers. "The queens around here go weak in the knees for the brothas with locs. Sit on down Kingman."

"Take it easy sister, I've never been bald."

"It's okay. The sistas are getting shaved too. I went through it too. I cried because I had a tight ass weave."

"I couldn't see you with a weave," Thomas said as he sat down admiring Akua closed-cropped hair.

"Chile, let me tell you…"

"I could get used to this look," Thomas said as he looked at his newly shaved head.

"When I was a barber many moons ago I used to charge thirty dollars for that cut. And you better had tipped."

They both laughed.

"Now for the real work." Akua got more serious. "When I leave I want you to take off all of your clothes including your shoes and put them into this plastic bag." Akua indicated the bag by the desk.

"You have a laundry service?"

"No we're burning them. If you check the dresser and closets you will find a few pieces of clothing, some undergarments, and shoes. Everything manufactured by Sankofans.

"Now after discarding your clothes I want you to take a shower with a special gel you will find in your bathroom shower. As you are taking your shower I want you to visualize that you are washing away the vestiges of the Machine Culture.

"Afterward, rest for a little while until we get you for brunch. I know you're not Vegan, but few of us touch meat. You'll be introduced to a nutritious Vegan meal."

"I'm looking forward to the meal. Thank you for everything."

Akua smiled. "We're family. That's how we roll."

Thomas was excited as he walked with Akua to the dining room. The shower seemed like it washed a lot of negative energy off of him. He couldn't remember the last time he slept so well.

When they got to the dining room, the people who came with Thomas were already there. There was a buffet to the side with assorted Vegan and raw food dishes. Thomas got a plate of Tofu chicken, raw seaweed, potato salad, and a biscuit.

As they ate they introduced themselves to each other.

TaKeisha was the sister with the braids and tattoos. She had come from one of DC's many housing projects. Though rough around the edges she had a decent wage job working at a mega grocery store. TaKeisha always looked to broaden her horizons. One day she happened to walk into a health food store where she saw a flier for a poetry reading at Afrikan Renaissance.

Morgan had been in corporate America since college working for a prominent WorldNet company. She had the townhouse, the car, and the credit score. Despite everything Morgan felt something was

49

missing from her life. She felt this way for years. Then one day she needed to get a book for her book club meeting. She made a wrong turn and happened to see Afrikan Renaissance. They didn't have the book but they had other things that caught her interest.

Harold was older than the others. He had been a manager at an auto plant until the depression came. When his plant closed, Harold lost his home, his wife, and his status. He lived on the streets since 2017. Somehow Harold managed to maintain his sanity. One day he happened to get a smoothie from a juice bar a block away from Afrikan Renaissance.

Thomas shared his story with the others. It was amazing how comfortable he was opening up to strangers.

After brunch the four went outside for the first time. Thomas got a better look at everything. They looked like they were in a valley. There were twelve houses he saw including the one he was in. There were other people standing around the houses. Some of the people had white clothing and shaved heads. Thomas still didn't see any children. Maybe the group didn't take children. That didn't make sense. Surely members of the group got married and had children. Auset interrupted Thomas's thoughts as she spoke to the entire group.

"I'm pleased that everyone seems to be settling in. Get some rest today and tomorrow you will be told the story of the Sankofa Collective."

FOURTEEN

Several people sat on blankets in a grassy hill near the houses. A Griot would tell the story of the Sankofa Collective. Akua explained to Thomas that instead of a sterile lecture, which was a left-brain modality, many important lessons were imparted in stories told in a relaxed atmosphere. This appealed to the right brain that facilitated memorization. The Griot telling the story of the collective was a small brother who looked to be in his late forties though Akua said the brother was approaching eighty. The Elder, Baba Kwabena, surveyed the one hundred odd Sankofans, old and new, before him. He began to speak in a powerful voice that belied his size.

The Sankofa Collective, our great nation, spanning the globe, with millions of citizens began in the mind of one man.

A man of vision.

Our Great Founder.

At the dawn of this century the world was in transition.

Wars of terror.

Wars for oil.

Wars for greed.

Wars against the poor and helpless.

Humanity was on the precipice of the abyss.

The Black man and woman in particular faced a dire future.

There were conventions and conferences.

Rom Wills

There were marches and protests.

There was legislation and debate.

Yet our people continued to march into the fire of impotence and irrelevance.

Our people cried for help.

One man stepped forward.

He was neither a politician nor a preacher.

He was not a scholar or activist.

He was not rich or famous.

He didn't own any material goods.

He was one thing and one alone: an Afrikan with the conviction that he could make a difference.

He envisioned a mass of Afrikans creating a global nation based on the principle of Sankofa – returning to the past in order to move forward.

But this didn't mean simply studying history and recreating one of myriad Afrikan cultures.

Sankofa, for the Great Founder, meant returning to our true selves as the Creator made us.

He didn't create a bunch of self-hating Negroes with fried hair and color contacts.

She didn't create a bunch of niggas elevating decadence to an art form.

Sankofa meant returning to our natural hair.

To our natural health.

To our natural ways of relating to ourselves.

To our Creator.

To our true selves as Afrikans.

Sankofa! Sankofa! Sankofa!

The Founder shared his vision with a small group of friends.

But these were not ordinary acolytes who basked in the light of charismatic speakers living fantasies of revolution before going back into the mundane day-to-day existence of the Machine Culture.

Nor were these activists known in the public eye as advocates of Afrikan liberation.

No these brothas and sistas were vendors and small business owners. A group of twelve that included a street vendor who sold books, a Vegan chef, a gardener, a T-Shirt designer and a house contractor. The Founder and the Twelve who believed in his vision.

Twelve plus one equals thirteen. Thirteen, the number of transformation.

It was thus that the Sankofa Collective, our great nation, was born.

They were initially one voice among many that agitated for everything from reparations to fair housing. A quiet voice. A voice that rather than yelling to the masses whispered in many ears.

Unlike others the Collective didn't ask for anything from those who represented true power.

Do for Self *was our anthem.*

The Founder and the Twelve pooled their resources to help one another build their businesses, one month at a time.

So a street vendor selling books opened a store in a shopping mall. A Vegan chef opened a small takeout place in a strip mall. A backyard gardener purchased an acre of land in which to plat crops. A T-Shirt designer produced a line of clothing with Afrikan themes. A house contractor fixed up an apartment building.

At the end of a year The Founder and The Twelve had began to build the economic infrastructure of our nation. Each business facilitated the creation of other businesses. As the bookstore grew and became two, then four, opportunities were created for book and magazine publishers, music companies, and artists. This created opportunities for printers, for distributors, for writers, and editors.

The Vegan café grew to create more cafes and then gourmet restaurants.

The one-acre farm, which became ten acres, one hundred acres, and then several farms, supplied food for the cafes and restaurants, as well as the growing chain of health food stores.

Thousands of jobs provided by the Collective for those who were proudly Afrikan.

This was merely the first phase as the Sankofa Collective still consisted of the Founder and the Twelve.

The year was 2010 when the Collective went into expansion. First those who worked for the businesses were offered membership. No one refused our invitation.

For those outside our businesses, the invitation only went to select Afrikan men and women.

Rom Wills

We invited carpenters and plumbers.

Electricians and brick masons.

We invited road builders.

We also invited architects, engineers, and scientists who were experts in alternate energy sources.

We had carefully and meticulously built up our economic foundation. Now it was time to physically build our nation.

The Founder and the Twelve had built up considerable financial resources. This money was used to purchase huge tracts of land in North and South America, the Caribbean and in Afrika. This land was purchased using front companies, foundations, and trusts.

We also purchased entire blocks of abandoned houses and buildings in major cities in the United States.

Our new architects designed homes and entire communities.

Our scientists developed alternative energy sources to power the homes.

We paved new roads. In a two-year period we built a global network of small communities.

Yet the houses sat empty.

The year was 2012, the year of the depression that changed everything.

It was time for phase three.

Allow me to digress. Despite the growth and power of the Collective by 2012, our membership numbered only in the thousands. We shunned the public media unlike other organizations.

The ONE thing we never established was a newspaper. We never issued press releases. There were no press conferences.

Even though our businesses had websites the term "Sankofa Collective" never appeared on the WorldNet or Internet as it was called then. So the average person, even if they were Afrikan-Centered, never heard of us. At the time it might not have mattered anyway.

An overwhelming majority of our people didn't have an interest in Afrikan culture beyond a superficial celebration of Kwanzaa.

They had jobs, homes in the suburbs, and social security. Even the unemployed could find a meal. America was good to our people, a few racist incidents notwithstanding. There was no reason to get into that Afrikan stuff.

Then the depression hit and formerly smug Blacks watched in tears as they received pink slips, received foreclosure notices, and watch their stock portfolios become worthless. It was then we began to populate our communities.

One by one Blacks walked through doors at bookstores, hair salons, cafes, and restaurants.

One by one Blacks became Sankofans.

Slowly people escaping the Machine Culture populated our new communities.

They came to communities like Garvey, slept in the rooms you are in now. Ate at the tables you eat at now. Sat on the grass you sit on now.

To Garvey they came.

To X they came.

To King they came.

To Muhammad, to Tubman, to Wells, to Toure, to Nkrumah, to Mumia.

They came to build a nation.

The Sankofa Collective!

Sankofa! Sankofa! Sankofa!

FIFTEEN

Thomas walked back to the house with Akua and the others. It was so incredible to him that such a large organization could be built and that there has been no mention of it in the media. He had read a special edition of *Newstime* that listed every single Black organization considered radical by the U.S. government. How come the Sankofa Collective wasn't mentioned?

Many thoughts ran through Thomas's mind as the group walked back to the house. As they got closer he saw a familiar person. Even though he tried to maintain his cool, a smile crept on his face, as he got closer to the house. The person stepped off the porch and spoke first.

"Brotha Thomas, I see you made it through the door." Malik embraced Thomas.

"Yes brother, I made it through."

"Now if we can work on that white boy accent," Akua said as she walked up and embraced Malik warmly. "Greetings Baba Malik."

Malik smiled broadly, "Can't resist can you Mama Akua! I still have to get used to being called Baba."

Thomas wondered what was that about.

"You mind if I borrow Thomas for awhile Mama Akua?" Malik asked. "I'll drive him around to show him the rest of Garvey."

"All right now. He still has some studying to do. Don't have him hanging out in the Club."

"It's cool sista. You know my Queen ain't playing that," Malik laughed. He turned to Thomas. "Let me show you where I live."

"I thought you lived in DC?" Thomas asked as they walked toward a small blue car.

"I did. I had to move down here."

"What about your job at MagnaCorp?"

"I quit. You know mail workers aren't bright enough to stay in good jobs."

Thomas laughed as they got to the car. "I've never seen this design before."

Malik opened the driver's side door. "It's a design by a Sankofan company out of Ghana. It's an electric car that will out perform anything out of Korea."

"Electric?" Thomas asked as he settled into the passenger seat. "I read an article that said the electric cars weren't viable."

"Thomas, one thing you have to learn is that the media is nothing but a propaganda organ for the oil companies that still rule this world. Well, maybe not the entire world," Malik chuckled.

Malik started the engine and Thomas was surprised at how quiet it was. Malik spoke as if he read Thomas's mind. "Yeah the car is quiet. We only use electric cars within our communities. We have gas cars for use when we go into the Machine Culture. All the energy we use is either electric or solar. Our water comes from wells and streams that run through our lands. We don't use state utilities for obvious reasons."

"The ride is incredible." Thomas felt comfortable as they drove on a tree lined small road. "Where are we going?"

"I'm going to show you the rest of Garvey."

"I thought we just left Garvey."

"That was just one part of Garvey. When the Collective first started each of the Twelve had a house built. They were able to buy more land as the Collective grew."

"So what's in the rest of Garvey?"

"Same thing as any small town. We have a town hall, a shopping mall, and a Club that has some of the best fruit drinks in the Collective. There is also a large residential area. Here we are."

As the car emerged out of the wooded road, Thomas surveyed the rest of Garvey. The place looked like a college campus, an Afrikan college campus. There were only a few cars on the streets, while hundreds of Sankofans walked in and out of different stores. He also saw a few small parks where people were reading books.

"I've noticed that Sankofans always seem to have a book in their hands," Thomas said.

"There is a saying among us that a Sankofan without a book either hasn't been born yet, has been knocked unconscious or is dead."

Thomas laughed. "It's amazing that this place looks like a college campus."

"As far as the government is concerned it is a college campus that belongs to a Bible School. The Redeemed Church of the Deliverer, one of our many front organizations, owns this land. If a spy satellite happens to take a picture of this area they would just think we're a church that takes Afrika day a little too far."

A question popped into Thomas's head but he decided it could wait. He had another question instead. "How are the Sankofa communities organized? Where is the capital?"

"The communities are both interconnected and self-sufficient. Each community is able to grow it's own food and manufacture its own products. I already mentioned we have our own power sources.

"As far as our government...The Founder and the Twelve represent the supreme leadership. They appoint specially trained administrators every five years to coordinate the worldwide activities of the Collective."

"Do you have elections?"

"It depends on the community. Each community has a Council of Elders who decides on a form of government. Most people are appointed to leadership positions. A few may be elected. We do it this way to prevent power struggles. Egos created by living in the Machine Culture are hard to suppress."

"Are y'all connected to each other through the WorldNet?"

"No, it would be a security risk. We've developed a sophisticated courier system to send messages between communities. Better than the U.S. Postal Service. We send the messages on encrypted discs."

"If you're not connected to the WorldNet what do you do about currency? The banks are connected to the Net."

"Well that's interesting. Within communities like Garvey we use our own currency. If we went to the Club I would purchase some smoothies and Mushroom Burgers with a credit card connected to a bank that serves only the Collective. Each community has an internal network.

"Now for our city communities they will use Sankofan dollars but also mainstream banks. Some of our city businesses are patronized by non-Afrikans, such as our restaurants. The money is deposited into the mainstream banks. Our dollar, by the way, goes further than the US dollar because our standard is the same as the Chinese Yen."

"Wow. It seems you thought of everything."

"We had no choice." Malik pulled into the parking lot next to what looked like a housing development. "We here."

Thomas noticed that there were plenty of trees. Tall trees which could obscure the community from the sky. He thought about what Malik said about spy satellites. The Sankofa Collective appeared to be very security conscious.

Rom Wills

"Where are we headed?" Thomas asked as he got out of the car.

"My house," Malik said as he closed his car door.

Thomas noticed that Malik didn't lock the car door. "You don't have a driveway?" Thomas saw people walking around, sitting on porches, or working in yards.

"We don't allow cars in our residential areas."

"Why not? The cars aren't noisy."

"No but accidents can always happen. We have to protect our most precious commodity."

"What's that?"

"We're coming up on it. Just listen."

Thomas got quiet and concentrated his hearing. At first the noise was faint, then as they walked the sound got louder. It was unmistakable. When they arrived at the source of the noise Thomas felt tears in his eyes. Children!

There were literally hundreds of children ranging from toddlers to pre-teens running around chasing each other and having a good time. He noticed several men and women watching or playing with children. Many of the women were visibly pregnant and many were breast-feeding infants.

Thomas looked beyond the playground and saw several teenagers playing a soccer game. In another part in a small park there were Sankofan children, doing what else? Reading books.

Malik spoke, "This is what it's all about. Our Watotos. Our children. Our future. We created our communities not just to escape the Machine Culture, but to raise our children in a safe environment. Young children aren't allowed in our city communities until they have gone through a rites of passage program.

"One of our biggest mistakes as a people was allowing our children to be raised in a hostile environment. Here we have schools designed to develop our Watotos to their highest potential. We don't give them drugs or put them in special education. We treat them the same way a gardener treats a prize winning rose bush. I'm going to be working as a teacher here."

"Where is here?"

"South Carolina. Most of our communities in the States are concentrated in South Carolina, Georgia, Alabama, Louisiana and Mississippi. We have communities in all states though and throughout the world."

"Why those five states in particular?"

Malik smiled, "You're not ready to hear about Phase Four. Let's just say you better get used to the idea of being a father. We discourage single people in the Collective. No playas and divas up in here. Most of what we're doing is family-orientated."

Thomas had an image of him and Ayanna playing with an infant.

Malik and Thomas finally made it to Malik's house, which was small and modest. Outside a pregnant sista was planting flowers. She smiled when she looked up at Malik.

"Thomas this is my wife, Nzinga. Nzinga, this is the brotha I told you about from MagnaCorp."

Nzinga embraced Thomas. "Welcome to Garvey brotha. Malik has told me a lot about you."

"I hope I have lived up to your expectations."

"All I expect you to be is Sankofan."

Thomas smiled. "I think I can handle that."

"Thomas," Malik said. "You have to try my Queen's barbecue gluten twists. They'll have you in heaven. Come on in."

They walked in and Malik asked Thomas to have a seat. Malik saw that Thomas had a question on his mind.

"What's on your mind Brotha Thomas?"

"I took in everything you and Baba Kwabena said. I know you have plenty of security measures. It still amazes me that an organization of this size can escape the attention of the government. I mean, I know you…we… have some type of intelligence service, but even the best organizations have defectors. What if an outsider puts two and two together?"

Malik looked at Thomas in all seriousness. "I'm not sure. It has to be something. I always wondered the same thing. Deep in my heart I worry about the one person who can unravel everything."

SIXTEEN

"I'm honored that someone in your position would talk with me personally." Ward McWhorter was sitting in the office of the Director of Homeland Security, Daniel Free. Free was a Black man in his fifties, a conservative who was well respected by all four of the political parties. Many people considered a Daniel Free a strong candidate for President of the United States, which according to rumors he was strongly considering a run in four years.

Ward initially brought his suspicions about Afrikan Renaissance to a friend at a Homeland Security field office. He didn't hear anything for two weeks and then all of sudden he was contacted and a meeting was set up with the Director himself. Ward always thought that there was more than met the eye with Afrikan Renaissance.

Daniel Free was relaxed as he spoke. "Mr. McWhorter...

"Ward."

"Ward. Tell me everything you suspect about Afrikan Renaissance."

Rom Wills

Ward told Daniel everything he knew and suspected about Afrikan Renaissance. Daniel raised his eyebrows when Ward mentioned that there may some type of Afrocentric underground. After Ward finished speaking it was Daniel's turn to talk.

"Ward, what I'm about to say is classified information. If you divulge this to the media or anyone else you will face dire consequences. Am I clear?"

Ward's face went ashen. "P-perfectly."

"Homeland Security has been aware of an Afrocentric underground for quite some time. This particular organization has existed for roughly thirty years. They are a cult with branches all over the world. They use sophisticated brainwashing techniques."

"I knew it!" Ward exclaimed.

"Calm down Ward. They are very dangerous but we have successfully infiltrated their group. In a few years they will be exposed."

"Thank God. How much do you know about them?"

"That's classified. We do know that they strong connections with several African and Caribbean governments."

"What can I do to help?" Ward asked eagerly.

Daniel looked at Ward for a few seconds. "Why are you so eager to help?"

"Mr. Free, I can't stand Blacks who try to pretend we're anything but Americans. Our history started here in this great country. I couldn't stand it when people would talk about these fictional West African kingdoms or try to pretend the Egyptians were Black. I hated when people called me African. I'm not African!"

Daniel thought that Ward looked like the ambassador from Senegal but he decided to keep it to himself. "Ward, you have helped enough. What you can do for us is keep this conversation to yourself. We will deal with this Afrocentric threat."

Ward stood up to leave. "Thank you. I have to say Mr. Free. It was an honor to meet you. You are an example of how good America is to Black people."

"Thank you, Ward. I do my best to repay America's kindness."

****

Daniel Free pulled into the driveway of his house in a gated community in Fairfax County, Virginia. He got out of his Mercedes and walked into his spacious home. He immediately went to his basement and walked to a door with a hand print lock. Pressing his hand against the scanner the door opened. Daniel walked in and the door closed behind him. This was Daniel's private room. This room didn't exist in the blueprints for the house.

The room had a red, black, and green flag painted on one wall and on the other wall there was a gold *Gye Nyame* symbol. On a small table there was a Sankofa wood sculpture. Daniel took off his shoes and sat cross-legged on the floor after lighting some Frankincense and Myrrh incense. This was the same ritual Daniel did whenever he encountered men like Ward. Poor Ward, he didn't realize his time on Earth would be cut short.

Daniel thought back to when he and the Founder decided to create the Sankofa Collective. They had been the best of friends, closer than brothers. They were politically astute and culturally aware students in high school. They were both sixteen when they came up with the idea of the Collective.

They took a year to develop the plan. Every aspect was outlined. Every move was planned out step by step. There was only one variable: the likelihood of discovery. They decided the best way to escape discovery was to have someone in the establishment. They didn't know anybody they could trust. They needed someone in place before the Collective got started. The purpose was to sabotage any investigation into Collective activities. They decided they could trust only themselves to do the job right. They decided to flip a coin to decide who would do what.

Heads. Daniel starts the Collective and the Founder would become a part of the establishment.

Tails. The Founder starts the Collective and Daniel joins the establishment.

Rom Wills

The coin is flipped.

Two destinies decided on a coin flip.

Tails.

The friends accept the result. No two out of three.

No one else would ever know what transpired not even members of the Collective.

Daniel accepts a scholarship to Harvard.

The Founder, despite being a straight "A" student, drops out of high school and becomes invisible to the system.

As Daniel sat on the floor he remembered what brought him and the Founder to their fateful decision. They were seven year olds in a housing project. They already experienced the conditions faced by Blacks everyday but there was one moment that defined their lives. They were watching a TV show about the Civil Rights movement when they saw clips showing the children in Birmingham being attacked with water hoses and dogs. At that moment Daniel and the Founder said in unison, "They will pay".

Daniel opened his eyes. He had learned one thing dealing with the politics of the establishment. The best way to lie sometimes is to mix in the truth. In fact, tell the truth, just not the whole truth. He wasn't lying when he told Ward the "Afrocentric Underground" would be exposed. What Daniel didn't say was that the "Afrocentric Underground" would expose themselves during the administration of a Black President.

One Year Later...

The man formerly known as Thomas Hunter sat at the desk of his small apartment in Garvey. He was about to go back into the Machine Culture for the first time in a long time. He was looking at newspaper clippings and articles from the past year. A couple of articles stood out amid the news of wars and poverty.

There was a story about Ward McWhorter being killed in a carjacking. It was unbelievable that Ward was shot six times point blank just for a car. The Machine Culture was indeed crazy.

Another article that stood out was about the Director of Homeland Security, Daniel Free. Even though there was a recent election people were already clamoring for Mr. Free to run for President in 2036.

The man formally known as Thomas Hunter laughed at the thought.

He put away the clippings and gathered his few belongings to hold him while he was in DC. It was time for him to leave.

****

"Baba Malik!" Ayanna could barely contain her excitement as she hugged and kissed Malik upon entering the café section of Afrikan Renaissance. "What are you doing here?"

"Just up to visit for a bit. I loved that last Vid you put out."

"Thanks Baba. How's your wife and daughter?"

"They're doing fine. How're you doing otherwise?"

"I'm doing well though I'm ready to leave DC and start a family. Just need the husband."

"Still haven't found the right one yet?"

"You know all Sankofan brothas are righteous but I haven't felt that chemistry yet."

"Well, I have a friend from Garvey I would like for you to meet. He's at a table over in the corner."

Ayanna walked with Malik over to the table. At first glance he was a Sankofan with nice locs and a beard. As she got closer she recognized his eyes. It was Thomas!

"Ayanna Toure…I would like for you to meet my good friend, Kwame Akoto."

Kwame stood up and took Ayanna's hand, "Peace Queen, I would like the honor of getting to know you."

"Stop blushing Ayanna," Malik smiled.

"Stop playing Baba." Ayanna turned to Kwame. "I would like the honor of getting to know you as well."

Kwame and Ayanna smiled broadly as they sat down to begin a new chapter in their lives.

Also By Rom Wills

Nice Guys and Players
Sexual Chemistry
Starting From Zero

www.romwills.com
Facebook.com/Willspublishing
Twitter: @romwills1

www.ingramcontent.com/pod-product-compliance
Lightning Source LLC
Chambersburg PA
CBHW020339130626
46549CB00003B/1216